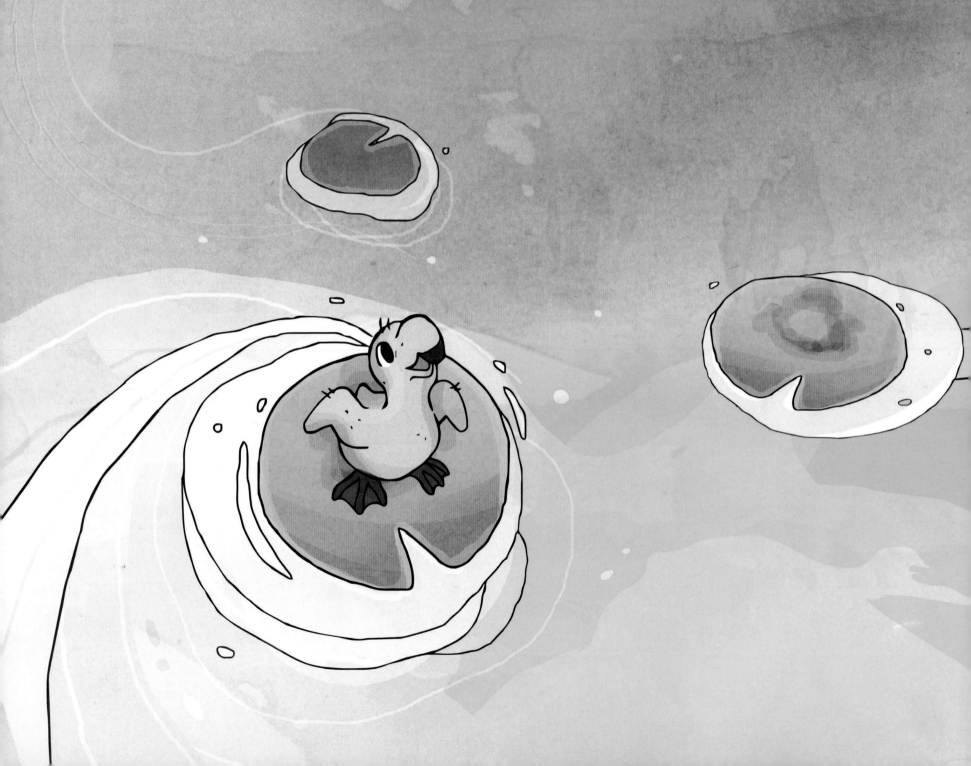

This book is given with love:

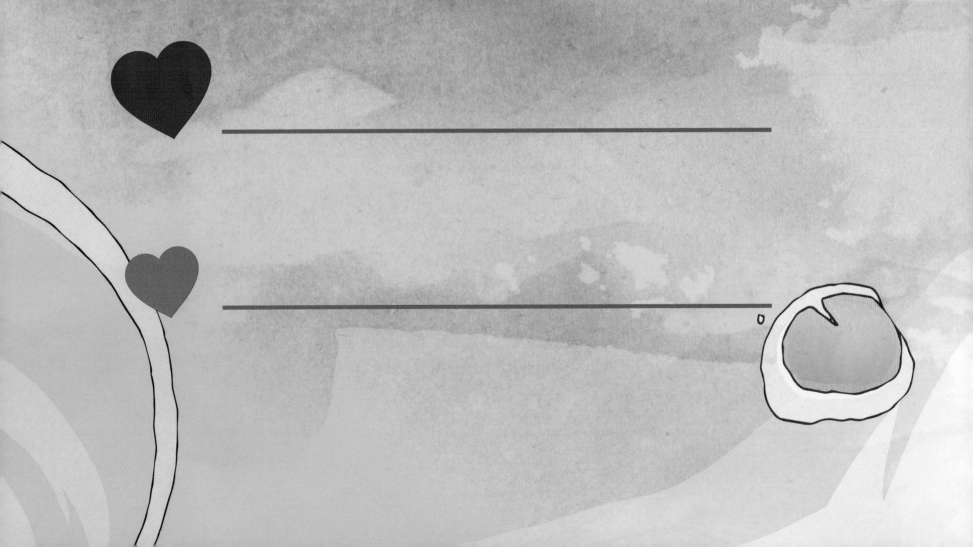

ISBN: 978-1-949474-49-7

Edition: June 2019

For all inquiries, please contact us at:

info@puppysmiles.org

To see more of our books, visit us at:

www.PuppyDogsAndIceCream.com

FIONA FLAMINGO

WRITTEN BY
Rachael Urrutia Chu

ILLUSTRATED BY
Kate Jeffery

On a beautiful sunny afternoon
where life was simply the best,
A little flamingo named Fiona
hatched from her egg in a nest.

Little Fiona grew up,

making lots of friends.

They played flamingo games

from days' start to days' end.

As the time passed,

the birds all became stronger.

They also got pinker,

and their feathers grew longer.

They turned pinker and pinker
with each feather they grew.
They got bigger and bigger
until some of them flew!

Fiona remained featherless,
until it happened one night...
She woke up with feathers
but they were bright...WHITE!

The other flamingos gasped
and stared at her in shock.

They couldn't believe what they were seeing
and wildly began to squawk.

Her friends looked at the white feathers

not knowing what to think,

"You're not the right color.

Flamingos are supposed to be PINK!"

With everyone shouting,
Fiona began to get scared.
She looked at her feathers,
and then she looked at theirs.

"You don't have to be so loud,

and please don't make a scene."

That's when Fiona started shaking,

and her feathers turned to...GREEN!

When her friends saw the change,
they squawked louder and meaner.
Fiona got more anxious,
and her feathers grew greener.

Her friends looked at the green feathers

not knowing what to think,

"Stop being so silly Fiona.

Flamingos are supposed to be PINK!"

"Oh no," said Fiona,

"This is worse than just bad..."

But her friends kept on squawking,

and then Fiona got mad.

"You're making me angry!"
She jumped and furiously said.
That's when Fiona started yelling,
and her feathers turned to...RED!

The flock became silent,
hoping things would get better,
But Fiona got madder,
and her feathers grew redder.

Her friends looked at the red feathers
not knowing what to think,
"Don't you think you should calm down now?
Flamingos are supposed to be PINK!"

They all rushed to hug her,

and now Fiona felt bad.

Her anger was fading,

but now she felt sad.

She whimpered and cried,
"I'm all mixed up in hue."
That's when Fiona started sobbing,
and her feathers turned to...BLUE!

The flock watched from afar,
and their concerns grew truer.

But Fiona just got sadder,
and her feathers grew bluer.

Her friends looked at the blue feathers

not knowing what to think,

"Just what kind of bird are you?

Flamingos are supposed to be PINK!"

No one could cheer her up,

so instead they stayed away.

That's when Fiona got lonely,

and her feathers turned to...GREY!

A young chick floated up,

with a gaze so pure and true.

"I hope my feathers change colors

when I'm as big as you!"

Fiona flashed a happy smile,
and her feathers erupted in color.

It was a surprise to everyone...

no feather was like any other!

PINK, WHITE, and GREEN,

RED, BLUE, and GREY...

She was every single color now,

and that's the way she'd stay!

The entire flock gathered around,
and Fiona gave a big wink.
"I guess we've all learned a lesson here...
Flamingos don't have to be PINK!"